Teacher's Pet

WRITTEN BY

Shawna Thomson

ILLUSTRATED BY

Tindur Peturs

What are you reading?
Is it that one we're reading in class?
Um, a chapter book.
No, I finished that one. I got this one at the library.

You finished it already?!

I'm not even going to read it. It's so boring.

Eyes up here, everyone! I am handing back your math tests on fractions from last week.

Most of you did a good job!

An A!
Nice work, Ellie!
Thanks, Rebecca!

Some of you need to see me after school so we can go over what you missed.

Of course you got an A. Teacher's pet.

Sorry I'm late, Rebecca!

One of these days I'll get an A in math like you, Ellie!

Hey, did you hear about the dance this weekend? Do you wanna go?
Sure, Ublu.

Sweet! I can't wait.

Are you going, Dana?
Yep!

Okay class, let's get started.

DANA
I'M NOT GOING WITH YOU NERDS THOUGH...

LATER THAT NIGHT, AT ELLIE'S HOUSE
How was school today?
Um, it was okay. I got my fractions test back.

Oh yeah, how did you do?

I got an A.

Ellie, that's awesome! I know you studied hard for that test.

Thanks! Let's eat!

Atii.
DINNER'S READY!

I don't care if Dana doesn't like me. I have my family and Ublu. I love spending time with them!

Thanks for helping me with dinner tonight, Ellie. It was delicious!
Mmm, it was!

Can I go on the computer for a bit, *Anaana*?
Atii, go ahead!

But remember, just half an hour.

1

DANA
SO SICK OF ALL THE NERDS AT MY SCHOOL, LIKE ELLIE! THEY GET AN A AND THINK THEY'RE BETTER THAN EVERYONE ELSE. NO WONDER SHE DOESN'T HAVE ANY FRIENDS!

ALICE
LOL SHE IS THE WORST!!!

MIALI
SUCH A NERD.
HOPE SHE'S READING THIS.

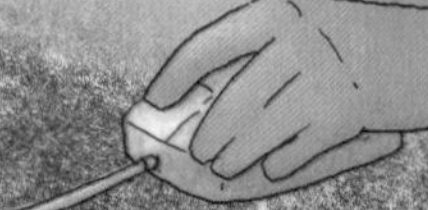

DANA
Dana, that's really mean. I don't think I'm better than you, or anyone. Can you delete that??
OMG YOU ARE SUCH A LOSER! NO WONDER NO ONE LIKES YOU! LOL

THE NEXT MORNING...

WHERE'S ALL YOUR FRIENDS, LOSER? OH YA, FORGOT YOU DON'T HAVE ANY...

THE NEXT DAY...

ELLIE
Thanks for the new earrings, Ublu! I love them!
NICE EARRINGS, TOO BAD YOU'RE SO UGLY...

FRIDAY, THE DAY OF THE DANCE...

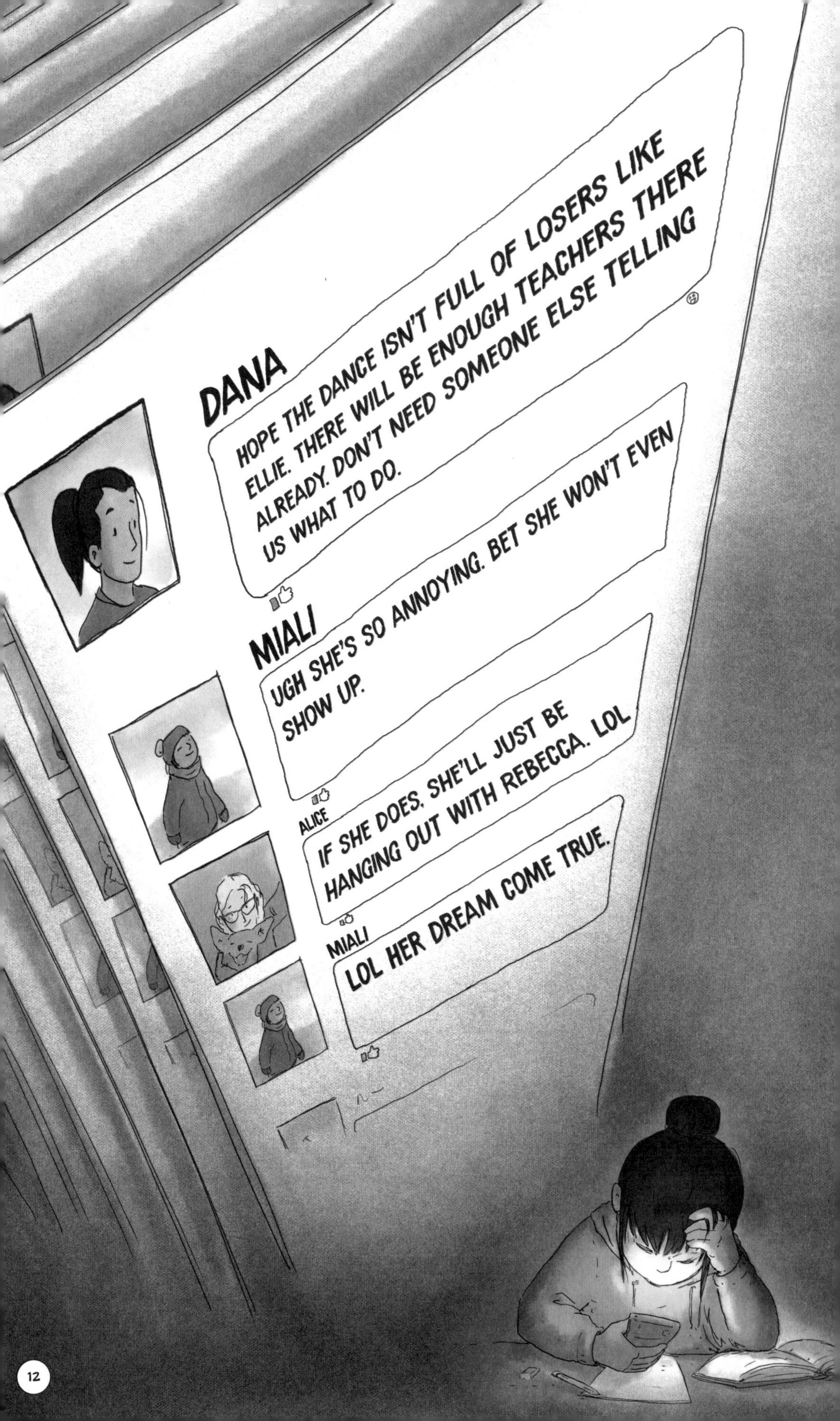
DANA
HOPE THE DANCE ISN'T FULL OF LOSERS LIKE ELLIE. THERE WILL BE ENOUGH TEACHERS THERE ALREADY. DON'T NEED SOMEONE ELSE TELLING US WHAT TO DO.
MIALI
UGH SHE'S SO ANNOYING. BET SHE WON'T EVEN SHOW UP.
ALICE
IF SHE DOES, SHE'LL JUST BE HANGING OUT WITH REBECCA. LOL
MIALI
LOL HER DREAM COME TRUE.

Ready to go?!

What's up?

Nothing, let's go!

Hey, there's Ellie. I wonder if she saw Dana's post...
I can't believe Dana wrote that!

Yeah, but she's right. Ellie never talks to anyone. So stuck up.
And a teacher's pet!

What's wrong?
Oh, it's nothing....

Did you go online after school?

Nah...my brother used all our WiFi gaming. My mom won't let us go on till next month.

Why?
It's nothing.
Great, at least one person didn't see Dana's post...

Who are you texting?
No one...
CAN'T BELIEVE U
SHOWED UP LOSER.
YOU DIDN'
WITH YOU
FRIEND,

Oh no...
another pos
from Dana.

DANA
THIS DANCE WOULD BE A LOT BETTER IF THERE WEREN'T SO MANY LOSERS HERE. WHY DID YOU EVEN COME, ELLIE? NO ONE WANTS YOU HERE.

Ellie, where are you going?

Who's been texting you all day?
It's nothing
don't worr
about it...

Then what's up with them?

I guess...Dana has been picking on me all week. She's been texting me and posting some pretty mean stuff online.

What?!

I tried to tell her to take it down, but she won't.
This is so mean!

She's just jealous that you're so smart. But she shouldn't be saying this stuff about you online! That's cyberbullying! Why didn't you tell me?
Cyberbullying?

Yeah, it's when someone is bullying you by posting things about you online.
You're right. I thought she'd stop if I didn't respond, but she's been bugging me all week. Ever since we got those math tests back.

NERD!
BET YOU WON'T EVEN GO TO THE DANCE BECAUSE YOU DON'T HAVE ANY FRIENDS.
GO CRY TO REBECCA
AFRAID TO WRITE BACK CAUSE YOU KNOW IT'S TRUE.
TEACHER'S PET LOL
This is awful!
LOL LOSER

I'm so embarrassed. I didn't want you to know people were saying those things in case you didn't want to be my friend anymore.

Maybe I am just a nerd with no friends...
I'll always be your friend!

Come on, let's get out of here. We can go to my house and watch a movie.
Okay.

I just don't know why she's picking on me....I wish I knew how to make her stop.
Dana is being a bully. I'm glad you didn't reply. There's no point in fighting with someone online.

But I think we should talk to someone. Maybe your sister? Or Rebecca?

I'm worried it will get worse if I tell Rebecca. Dana already thinks I'm a teacher's pet.

It doesn't matter what she thinks! When someone is treating you like this, you shouldn't keep it to yourself. It will just make you feel worse.

You're right. Maybe I will talk to Rebecca at school tomorrow...

I'll come with you, if you want.

Really?
Of course!

Thanks, Ublu. You're such a good friend.

ON MONDAY, AT SCHOOL...
Ready?
I think so...

What is Dana doing in there?

I'm worried, Dana. This is the second math test you've failed.

I know.

My mom is so mad at me. I don't know what she'll do if I fail the next one.

You can always come to me for extra help after school.

I have to go right home after school to make dinner for my little brothers and sisters.

My mom is always working late.
Maybe you could do some extra work at home?

It's always so loud at my house. So many kids around.

I can't focus. The homework is too hard. I don't understand the problems and then I just get frustrated.

Don't worry. We're going to work together to find a way to improve your grades.

I hope so. My mom says if I'm no good at school, I might as well be home watching my siblings. I really don't want to have to quit school.

Let's get out of here.
Don't you want to talk to Rebecca?
I'll talk to her later...

THAT NIGHT AT ELLIE'S HOUSE...
Ellie, can you pass me the flour?

Hellllooo? Earth to Ellie!
Sorry, what?

I asked you to pass me the flour. Like, three times.
Oh right...

Is something wrong? Seems like you have something on your mind.

I actually kind of have a problem. And I don't know what to do about it.

I find it helps to talk our problems out with someone. It helps you think about them when you say them out loud.
Okay...

...well, the past couple of days Dana has been really mean to me. She has been posting really mean stuff online.

And she's been sending me these nasty text messages.

Oh, Ellie. This is awful. I can't believe she's been bullying you.
And all these other kids commenting... they've been bullying you, too.

Why didn't you tell me?
I didn't want to tell anyone. I was so embarrassed. I thought maybe I was being stuck up and didn't have any real friends...

Not at all, Ellie. Sometimes people say things online that they would never say in person. That's why so many people are commenting. They feel braver and more powerful because they don't have to say things to you in person and see how they are hurting you.

But bullying is still bullying, even if it's online.
I know. Ublu told me about cyberbullying. She was going to help me talk to Rebecca about it, but then...

What happened?

Well, we went to talk to her after lunch, but Dana was already in there. She was talking to Rebecca about how she is having trouble in school. She said that her mom gets really mad at her when she gets bad grades. And if she doesn't get better grades, her mom might even take her out of school.

Oh no...how did it make you feel hearing Dana say that?
I actually felt bad for her. Like...maybe she's not nice to me because no one is nice to her at home.

Bullying is never okay. A lot of times, the person doing the bullying is doing it to feel powerful because they feel unsure or uncomfortable with other parts of their life. They want to feel like they have control over something in their life.

Yeah, I guess so. Dana failed that math test last week. She saw that I got an A, and that's when she started picking on me.

I thought she was just jealous, but I guess it's more than that.

I'm glad you told me, Ellie. Even if Dana is having a hard time, it doesn't give her the right to treat other people badly.
Yeah, I wish I had told you sooner. I feel so much better talking about it.

You can tell me anything, Ellie!

So, are you still going to talk to Rebecca?

No...I think I want to talk to Dana. Maybe I'll send her a message...

Maybe you should speak to her in person? Sometimes people feel like they can say things that they don't really mean online because they can't actually see who they are talking to.

Do you know what I mean?

That's a good point. I'll try to talk to her at school tomorrow.

Thanks, Maggie.
I'm glad you talked to me, Ellie.

AT SCHOOL THE NEXT DAY...

Are you sure about this?
Yeah, I'm sure.

Hey Dana...

What do you want?
I want to say that you have said some pretty mean things about me online.

Especially when everyone else started commenting on it.

Okay??

And those text messages were really hurtful. I don't think it's fair for you to make fun of me for being a good student.
Yeah, well...

I felt like I really didn't deserve any friends. I've been so sad all week. Every time I saw a message, I didn't even want to come to school. What's the point of working hard and studying when nobody likes you?

I was just kidding around. I didn't think you'd take it so seriously.

It didn't seem like you were kidding.

Or those other kids commenting on your posts. I don't get why you decided to pick on me.
You wouldn't get it.

You don't know what I have going on.
No, I don't.

But you don't know what I have going on either. I'm lucky. I have a good sister and friend who helped me remember that I am loved. But if I didn't... I would still be sitting at home, believing everything you said. And I might think that for the rest of my life.

I didn't think of that...

I didn't think at all. I just saw that you were happy and got so mad that you could be happy and I couldn't.

Why can't you be happy?

You're just a...a...

Ugh! Things have really sucked lately. School has gotten so hard, and I have to do everything at home. My mom is so mad at me all the time.

She said if I'm not getting good grades, I should just quit school and get a job instead.
Well, maybe I could help you with that.

Help me get a job??

No. I can help you study so you can get a better grade on the next test and stay in school.
Do you really think so?

For sure. My sister taught me a bunch of tricks that make math easier to understand. I can show you, too. I wouldn't get such good grades without help or somewhere quiet to study.

It's okay to ask for help, you know...

Ellie, I'm really sorry about what I posted online. I was angry and...I made a mistake. My words really must have hurt you. You're actually pretty cool, and way nicer than a lot of people I know.

Thanks, Dana.

What are you doing with that?
I'm taking those posts down. And...I'm going to write an apology, too.

Thanks, Dana. I'll see you later?
Sounds good!

Dana

Pretty glad Ellie asked me to study. Got a B on my math test and some new friends 🙂

10 👍